Billy Bishop Goes to War

BILLY BISHOP GOES TO WAR

a play by John Gray with Eric Peterson

Talonbooks · Vancouver · 1981

Published with the assistance of the Canada Council.

Talonbooks
P.O. Box 2076, Vancouver, British Columbia V6B 3S3
Tel: (604) 444-4889; Fax: (604) 444-4119; Internet: www.talonbooks.com

Printed and bound in Canada by Hignell Printing.

Eighth printing: October 2000

Talonbooks are distributed in Canada by General Distribution Services, 325 Humber College Blvd., Toronto, Ontario, Canada M9W 7C3; Tel.:(416) 213-1919; Fax:(416) 213-1917.

Talonbooks are distributed in the U.S.A. by General Distribution Services Inc., 85 Rock River Drive, Suite 202, Buffalo, New York, U.S.A. 14207-2170; Tel.:1-800-805-1083; Fax:1-800-481-6207.

Canadian Cataloguing in Publication Data

Gray, John, 1946-
    Billy Bishop goes to war

    ISBN 0-88922-196-0

    1.Bishop, William A., 1894-1956—Drama.
    I. Peterson, Eric, 1946-   II. Title
PS8563.R39B5   C812'.54   C82-091045-7
PR9199.3.G73B5

Preface

Billy Bishop Goes to War was born out of a nasty case of the Three B's of Canadian Theatre — Broke, Bored and Branded. Broke, because it was 1976 and there was not much work. Beating a trail from one one-hundred seat theatre to another is the usual lot of the Canadian theatre artist. Consequently, he is always broke. Bored, because our leaders, the Old Warriors of Canadian Nationalism, were in a rut. Audiences were getting ugly and scarce. But being Broke and Bored did not prevent us from being Branded as Canadian Nationalists, and, therefore, unfit for the more cosmopolitan world of the Regional Theatres. And so, we come full circle again, back to Broke — and the landlord turns off the heat.

It was at this time that Eric Peterson lent me a book called *Winged Warfare*. We were in Ottawa at the time, performing for Theatre Passe Muraille. Ottawa is one of the few Canadian cities in which the all-Canadian bookstore is a major entertainment resource. *Winged Warfare* was written by a twenty-one-year-old pilot named Billy Bishop and it contained a cool account of his first six kills during World War I. A little research indicated that before the war was over, he had upped his total to seventy-two. As representatives of a generation of Canadians who had never been anywhere near a war, we regarded the man with apprehension and curiosity. Was he a homicidal maniac? What was going on in that war? What was it like to be a Canadian then? Why were more top aces Canadian than any other nationality? As citizens of a relatively pacifist country, what was it about our nature that made us bold and daring whenever we became involved in a foreign war? What did all this have to do with our colonial heritage, our sense of inadequacy when it comes to our position in the English-speaking world? What was the experience of two generations before us whose lives were defined and shaped by war? Eric and I talked about these things for about a year in our favourite snooker halls and beer parlours — in between trips to the Military Archives to do research.

In January, 1978, I started writing and by March, I had a draft of a play that was almost as long as the war itself. Eric read it and approved. The Old Warriors of Canadian Nationalism read it. They approved. Theatre Passe Murraille gave us some workshop money, and Tamahnous Theatre got a commitment from the Vancouver East Cultural Centre for a production in the fall. With dreams of steady employment to inspire us, we set to work.

One choice we made: *Billy Bishop* would take its narrative form from a phenomenon I noticed while playing the barn circuit of Southwestern Ontario. Playing on stages where you had to kick the cowpies aside while crossing the boards, I noticed that Canadians don't much like listening in on other people's conversations. They think it's impolite. This plays havoc with the basic convention of theatre itself, so what do you do? Well, you drop the fourth wall and you simply talk to the audience. They tend to relax a bit because they are in an arena whose aesthetics they understand: the arena of the storyteller. A dogfight can be a tricky number to stage, and the sky is a hard thing to evoke with a roof over your head. But to a good storyteller anything is possible, and Eric is a wonderful storyteller.

Another choice: only two of us would do it. Eric would play all the parts and I would play the music; Eric would be the mouth and I would be the hands. That way, we got to keep all the money. Besides, one-man shows were all the rage in those days, times being what they were.

Billy Bishop Goes to War opened in Vancouver around Remembrance Day in 1978. The fact that there was a newspaper and a postal strike on didn't make November the best month for a premiere, but response was good and we were held over for two weeks. We seemed to have tapped a well of experience that had been hidden for years. Veterans from both wars came backstage to tell us stories, to talk about the ironic position of being a colonial in a British war; to express their ambivalence about their own survival in a war where so many of their friends died. This response was a source of tremendous relief to Eric and me. Our one fear was that someone would come backstage and say to us, "You're wrong. You got it all wrong. That's not the way it was at all."

Sometime during the holdover in Vancouver, a tall stranger came backstage. He was an American and he was smoking a cigar. He wore a sheepskin coat, had grey hair and the smile of a country doctor. His name was Lewis Allen. He was a producer; then, the co-producer of *Annie*. *Annie* was making the profit of an oil sheikdom at the time and he said that he thought *Billy Bishop* deserved to go to Broadway too. He would get his partner Mike Nichols to look at it. That's a good one, we thought. We entertained the fantasy for a few minutes, then left for the bar and forgot all about it.

We were feeling good. The Cultural Centre had arranged a two-week run in Saskatoon, a tour of Southwestern Ontario and a run at Theatre Passe Muraille. Even the Regional Theatres were beginning to nibble. We might work until the spring. Maybe buy a car. We were as happy in December of 1978 as any Canadian theatre artist can be. We had work; we had a show that didn't bore us; we had audiences who wanted to see our play, who gave us standing ovations. We were being paid.

Touring Canada in mid-winter, one encounters a lot of snow. A lot of snow and a lot of viruses. Every acting school in the country should teach a course entitled "Performing While Sick" because their students are going to be doing a lot of that. In Saskatoon, we learned how to perform with a bad cold. In Owen Sound, it was the flu. In Listowel, Ontario, it all came together in a kind of winter fugue. Eric had the flu; I had a cold—and there was a blizzard so bad that traffic from Kitchener had been stopped. This meant that the risers which the audience were to sit on didn't arrive, nor did the stage. And we were performing in an old railway station. We looked bad. That is, we looked bad if you could see us at all. Watching the show was like trying to get a peek at the scene of an accident. Those who did get a glimpse recoiled at the sight of two broken men croaking their way through a play, accompanied by a piano with six important keys missing. It was an evening to remember. But we got through the show. Once you're out there, it seems there's no alternative, so you go on. The audience applauded sympathetically and left. We collapsed backstage, calling for the antibiotics we had come to know and love.

In walked Mike Nichols. How he had got from New York to Listowel in a blinding snowstorm was a mystery to us. Perhaps he hired a personal snowplough. But there he was, looking just like he did on the cover of *Time*. He said that he liked the show. He said that he intended to bring it to New York. When he left, the snow swirled around his Vicuna coat like fog around a genie. We stared after him, wondering if the fever was worse than we thought. But Mike left something behind with us: the idea that we might become rich and famous. It was winter. It was Canada. What were the odds?

In theory, we all belittle the coarser rewards of life, but

it's usually sour grapes. When the prospects of riches and fame are actually dangled in front of us, we are in there like rats up a drainpipe. I've seen New York or Hollywood bring on many a pair of sunglasses in my life. We were no exception. Visions of limousines, handsome West Side suites, Piaget watches, dinners at Elaine's and smart Italian suits came to mind. Before you pass judgement, let's face it, most of us get into theatre for childish, silly reasons. You start out thinking that being in the theatre will make you an interesting person. I myself got interested in the theatre in the belief that women there would be looser than the general female populace. But after you have been working for a while, you find yourself just as boring as ever and your chances of scoring remain the same. So you replace an improbability with a complete absurdity: you dream about becoming a star. It is a rare person who knows that working in the theatre will not make you anything other than what you already are. And so you plod on, hoping against hope that one morning you'll wake up, read the reviews and realize that you've become glamorous and witty and cosmopolitan and rich. And you accomplish little, because when a dream of *being* takes hold, there is little room for thoughts of *doing*.

By the time we hit Toronto, we had become Top of the Pops. It's really amazing the extent to which Yankee acceptance affects Canadian prestige. Suddenly, *Billy Bishop* had become the show that Mike Nichols liked. This was the Canadian show that was going to Broadway. Overnight, a modest little work by and for Canadians had become a Hot Property. Newspaper articles, reviews, interviews all centred around the fact that we were going to Broadway. Were we excited? Would our play be a hit? Would it fail? How would we feel if it failed? There was never a word about the show itself; no interest in what it meant, what it was trying to say about war, about heroes, about Canada, about life. All that mattered was that we were going to Broadway. Would it make us rich and

9

famous? It was as if we'd suddenly switched careers. We were no longer Canadian performers. We were athletes on our way to the Olympics. Would we win or lose? Would we cure or confirm for the National Inferiority Complex?

Canadians have long existed with the suspicion that we have something missing in our chromosomal make-up when it comes to art; that there is some wishy-washy component in our gene structure that makes us incapable of strong artistic statement. This is our colonial heritage at work. We export natural resources and we import culture. That is our lot in life. When a Canadian work goes abroad, it is a little like an Indian running for Prime Minister. Our cultural inadequacy makes the odds for success rather long.

Still, I must say, the whole thing was very good for business. Interest from the Regional Theatres blossomed. Neither Eric nor I had worked in a Regional Theatre before. A tour of Regional Theatres was arranged for the following fall and winter. You see, government cutbacks and the demand for more Canadian plays had come at the same time. And what could be cheaper than a Canadian play with two actors? Then we were to go to Washington, D.C. for a tryout at the Arena Stage. Then we were to go to Broadway. Over a year's worth of work for us; we who had never run a show for more than six weeks of our lives. And a carrot on the end of the stick as well: New York.

I don't want to appear ungrateful for the opportunities that were presented to us, but we really weren't ready for this. We had barely got used to the idea of steady work when suddenly we were an international property with Canada's theatrical self-esteem in our care. For us, the future was full of peril. Terrible images came to mind: an anvil suspended above our heads ready to fall at any moment. We were like straight men in some monstrous slapstick comedy, for if there is such a thing as success, then there must be the opposite. Would we be heroes — or would we be bums? In the world in which we found ourselves, there was no middle ground, for Canadians reserve their greatest contempt for artists who fail abroad.

However, one adapts. One evolves. Some new plumage; an extra toe, but you cope. And cope we did — on a six months tour of the Regionals where we were to find what we had been missing all those years: the audience that goes to a hit show because it's the thing to do. It's a souvenir hunt. The fact that you saw such and such will make wonderful dinner conversation for days to come. "I saw *Billy Bishop Goes to War*. It's going to Broadway, you know."

The winter went by. We played Ottawa, Montreal, Halifax, Kingston, Hamilton, Kitchener, London, St. Catherines, Edmonton and Calgary. More snow fell on our heads; more viruses passed through our systems. Perhaps human beings were invented to transport viruses from one place to the next? Then there were the interviews. How does it feel to be a success? What's it like to be finally working in the bigtime? We never told them the truth. It wasn't newsworthy. We were being educated and education is expensive. We were learning that there was no such thing as easy money; we were learning just what kind of a meatgrinder you had to go through to get your sausage.

In March, 1980, we headed for the Arena Stage in Washington, D.C. Mike Nichols filled us in on the difference between the Canadian and the American aesthetic. To begin with, our little set with its roll drop and miniature plane simply would not do. For Canadians, this set gave the play a comic and human perspective in keeping with the hero. For Americans, the set was puny. When your American spectator pays upwards of twenty bucks a ticket, he wants to see equally conspicuous consumption on the part of the play. Our toy plane became a full-sized plane. The roll drop went and was replaced by a hydraulic lift, a smoke machine and triple the number of lighting instruments. Instead of forty thousand dollars, the budget was now three hundred thousand dollars. But we were still a modest little show.

We opened well. We received raves from the Baltimore and Washington papers, and, wonder of wonders, from *The New York Times*. Success seemed near at hand. However, we wondered just what it was audiences were seeing when they saw the show. I mean, these were Americans we were playing to, not Canadians. The difference between the two audiences was never so apparent as the night we were sitting in our underwear after the show when in walked the heads of the F.B.I., the C.I.A., the Joint Chiefs of Staff, the Air Force, along with Hodding Carter, the President's Press Secretary. These guys can make you feel real small, particularly when you're half naked. In any case, they pumped our hands, slapped our backs and said that they loved the show — without reservation. This gave us pause. We had been hoping for a little more appreciation of irony, but Americans, it seems, aren't into irony. In America, when you address a subject such as War, you're either for it or agin it. And when your hero is a military man, he is either a good guy or a bad guy. So when it came to *Billy Bishop*, which does not address itself to the issue of whether or not war is a good thing or a bad thing, we became pro-war by default. As a result, to the liberal press, we were bad guys, a disturbing harbinger of violent things to come. And to the conservative press, we were good guys, reassessing the military man without simplistic sixties judgements. Because popular mythology at the time had it that America was turning right, it was thought that we had hit just the right note for the times. For us, we were never sure whether or not we had hit the note that we wanted to hit. This was our first encounter with the American penchant for obscuring an issue by simplifying it beyond belief. As Canadians who tend to be paralyzed by the complications of life, we found all this a little strange.

But then again, who really cares about the content? How many people leave a play asking what it meant? Isn't it more important whether or not it was fun, whether or not it was skilfully produced, whether or not it was a hit, whether or not it was going to make its participants rich and famous? With no serious discussion of content among either audiences or press, an artist finds himself in a vacuum where ideas have no power. In a society where ideas are effectively robbed of their power, either by disinterest, greed, ignorance or decadence, an artist abandons the pursuit of an idea in favour of the pursuit of money. He is woven into the fabric of the capitalist system. By the time we reached New York, our little play, despite its original meaning, had become an expression of our desire to become rich and famous. *Billy Bishop Goes to War* had become an expression of the American Dream.

A Canadian never feels more Canadian than when he is in the United States. And these two Canadians were beginning to weary of the American Dream. In fact, we had taken to flying to Canada for a few days now and then, like divers coming up for air. And, to continue the metaphor, it seemed we were in a whirlpool that began to spin faster and faster. We were introduced to a great many rich and famous people in those months and we learned something about them. First of all, rich and famous people tend to come in pairs. The only way a rich and famous person can *feel* rich and famous is by hanging around with other rich and famous people. Rich and famous people tend to be very frightened of *not* being rich and famous. They are constantly looking over their shoulders to see if their riches and fame have decreased any. Another thing: only a certain number of people can be rich and famous. Somebody has got to fail. The whole thing is now in perspective. In the search for riches and fame, you will either succeed or fail. If you fail, you will be disappointed. If you succeed, you will be frightened. Take your pick.

Billy Bishop Goes to War opened at the Morosco Theatre on May 29, 1980. It received a standing ovation and rave reviews from eighty percent of the critics. The party at Sardi's was a huge success, with glittering people everywhere, and Andy Warhol, the Samuel Pepys of

Gotham, snapping Polaroids of everyone for posterity. When we walked back to our hotel at four o'clock in the morning, New York wasn't a city of filth, decay, bag ladies, derelicts and junkies. It was a magic city — a magic city where childish and greedy dreams come true.

The next morning, our producers were talking about closing the show. Nobody was buying tickets. "What happened?" the anguished Canadian press wanted to know. Was it a muddy review from the *Times*? Was it that the show was too small for the Broadway stage? Was the show not as good as we had thought? Was there really something missing from the Canadian chromosomal make-up? Were Canadians really inferior? Canadians take failure on Broadway much more seriously than Americans do. Americans know that hardly anything ever succeeds on Broadway — maybe about one show in a hundred. And we Canadians have put far less than one hundred shows on Broadway. It's a tremendous longshot. But this explanation is far too simplistic and pragmatic for the Canadian press. It doesn't address itself to the National Inferiority Complex. We still have interviewers asking, "What happened?" as though we were two runners who had failed to post their best times at the Olympics, and so, had let their country down.

What had happened was that our American producers had made a miscalculation. They were betting that rave reviews and the name of Mike Nichols, tastemaker to Broadway, would be enough to draw the huge grosses that were necessary to survive on a Broadway stage. They had thought that if they loved a play, Americans would love a play — even a Canadian play. They were wrong. Of course, if *Billy Bishop* were a British play, the job of selling it would have been tough, but possible. America has long had a love-hate relationship with Britain. Britain is the country it fought to achieve its independence; it was the country it eventually replaced as muscleman of the Western World. And Americans have a National Inferiority Complex too. They are afraid that even with all their technological, financial and military achievements, they have still not become a civilized country. Americans are afraid they are Rome to Britain's Greece. And admiration, envy and fear can combine to make a British success in America possible.

But a Canadian play? Forget it! Americans don't want to see two unknown Canadians perform a play about an unknown Canadian war hero who fought in a war that America did not win. Not with *Barnum* across the street. How good the play was was irrelevant, as were the reviews and the awards. Americans simply weren't buying it. It took our producers a few months and an unprecedented move to off-Broadway, where we should probably have been to begin with, before they admitted defeat. Rich and Famous, those two sirens, were finally silent.

When we left New York in August for the Edinburgh Festival, which was another story entirely, our parting was amicable. We have friends in New York and Mike Nichols jokingly offers to mis-produce anything I write. I sometimes think that education has more to do with the loss of illusions than with the acquisition of knowledge. If that is true, we received more education in four months in New York than in seven years at university. The tuition was high, but the school gave good value. Our experience in New York has given me the suspicion that, in fact, it may be better to give than to receive; that perhaps it is more difficult for a rich man to enter the kingdom of heaven. It seems that the greater our so-called international success became, the more we longed for audiences like those first few thousand souls who braved strikes, snow, viruses and lousy sightlines to see our little play about Billy Bishop. Perhaps theatre is a very simple activity in which a group of people get together to focus on what is best about themselves.

Eric and I would like to thank all those who helped along the way. Some of the names that would fill a small telephone directory are: Lewis Allen, Martin Bragg, Col.

Dode Clark, CP Air, Ross Douglas, Haig Farris, David Gropman, Beverlee Larsen, George Miller, Mike Nichols, Lorna Gail Peterson, Jay Presson-Allen, Cedric Smith, Ken Smith, Tommy Smith, Kay Staley, Ronald Stern, Paul Thompson, Jennifer Tipton, Paul Williams, Jackie Willis-O'Connor and Chris Wootten and all his colleagues at the Vancouver East Cultural Centre.

Billy Bishop Goes to War is dedicated to all those who didn't come back from the war, and to all those who did and wondered why.

John Gray,
Vancouver, B.C.
December, 1981.

Billy Bishop Goes to War was first produced by the Vancouver East Cultural Centre in association with Tamahnous Theatre at the Vancouver East Cultural Centre in Vancouver, British Columbia on November 3, 1978, with the following cast:

Narrator/Pianist John Gray

Billy Bishop, Upperclassman
Adjutant Perrault, Officer
Sir Hugh Cecil, Lady St. Helier
Cedric, Doctor, Instructor
General John Higgins, Tommy } Eric Peterson
Lovely Helene, Albert Ball
Walter Bourne, German
General Hugh M. Trenchard
Servant, King George V

Directed by John Gray
Set and Lighting Design by Paul Williams
Music and Lyrics by John Gray

During 1980 and 1981, "Squadron 86" company of *Billy Bishop Goes To War* performed in over fifty-five Canadian cities and appeared at the 1981 Bermuda Festival. The cast was:

Narrator/Pianist Ross Douglas

Billy Bishop and
the seventeen other } Cedric Smith
characters

Act One

The lights come up slowly on BILLY BISHOP
and the PIANO PLAYER, who sits at the piano.
They are in an Officer's Mess.

BISHOP AND PIANO PLAYER: *singing*
　　We were off to fight the Hun,
　　We would shoot him with a gun.
　　Our medals would shine
　　Like a sabre in the sun.
　　We were off to fight the Hun
　　And it looked like lots of fun,
　　Somehow it didn't seem like war
　　At all, at all, at all.
　　Somehow it didn't seem like war at all.

　　　BILLY BISHOP speaks to the audience. He is a
　　　young man from Owen Sound, Ontario. His
　　　speech pattern is that of a small town Canadian
　　　boy who could well be squealing his tires down the
　　　main street of some town at this very moment.

BISHOP: *to the audience*
I think when you haven't been in a war for a
while, you've got to take what you can get. I
mean, Canada, 1914? They must have been
pretty desperate. Take me, for instance. Twenty
years old, a convicted liar and cheat. I mean,
I'm on record as the worst student R.M.C.
...Royal Military College in Kingston,
Ontario....I'm on record as the worst student
they ever had. I join up, they made me an
officer, a lietuenant in the Mississauga
Horse. All I can say is they must have been
scraping the bottom of the barrel.

BISHOP AND PIANO PLAYER: *singing*
We were off to fight the Hun,
Though hardly anyone
Had ever read about a battle,
Much less seen a Lewis gun.
We were off to fight the Hun
And it looked like lots of fun,
Somehow it didn't seem like war
At all, at all, at all.
Somehow it didn't seem like war at all.

BISHOP: *to the audience*
Yeah, it looked like it was going to be a great
war. I mean, all my friends were very keen to
join up, they were. Not me. Royal Military
College had been enough for me. Now the
reason I went to R.M.C. is, well...I could ride
a horse. And I was a great shot. I mean, I am a
really good shot. I've got these tremendous eyes,
you see. And R.M.C. had an entrance exam
and that was good because my previous
scholastic record wasn't that hot. In fact, when I

suggested to my principal that, indeed, I was going to R.M.C., he said, "Bishop, you don't have the brains." But I studied real hard, sat for the exams and got in.

He imitates a R.M.C. Officer.

Recruits! Recruits will march at all times. They will not loiter, they will not window shop. Recruits! Recruits will run at all times when in the parade square. Recruits! Recruits will be soundly trounced every Friday night, whether they deserve it or not.

As himself.

I mean, those guys were nuts! They were going to make leaders out of us, the theory being that before you could learn to lead, you had to learn to obey. So, because of this, we're all assigned to an upperclassman as a kind of, well...slave. And I was assigned to this real sadistic S.O.B., this guy named Vivian Bishop. That's right, the same surname as me, and because of that, I had to tuck him into bed at night, kiss him on the forehead and say, "Goodnight, Daddy!" I mean, it's pretty hard to take some of that stuff seriously. One of my punishments: I'm supposed to clean out this old Martello Tower by the edge of the lake. I mean, it's filthy, hasn't been used for years. Now I do a real great job. I clean it up real well. This upperclassman comes along to inspect it.

UPPERCLASSMAN:
What's this in the corner, Bishop?

BISHOP:
    That?

He has another look.

That's a spider, Sir.

UPPERCLASSMAN:
    That's right, Bishop. That's a spider. Now you
    had orders to clean this place up. You haven't
    done that. You get down on your hands and
    knees and eat that spider.

BISHOP: *to the audience*
    I had to eat that spider in front of all my
    classmates. You ever have to eat a spider? In
    public? I doubt it. Nuts! Now, whenever I'm not
    happy, I mean, whenever I'm not having a
    really good time, I do one of three things: I get
    sick, I get injured or I get in an awful lot of
    trouble. My third year at R.M.C., I got into an
    awful lot of trouble. This friend of mine,
    Townsend, one night, we got a bottle of gin, eh?
    And we stole a canoe. Well, we'd arranged to
    meet these girls on Cedar Island out in Dead
    Man's Bay. Well, of course, the canoe tips over.
    Now, it's early spring, really cold. We get back
    to shore somehow and we're shivering and
    Townsend says to me, "Bish, Bish, I'm going to
    the infirmary. I think I got pneumonia." And
    I'm sitting there saying, "Well, whatever you do,
    you silly bugger, change into some dry clothes."
    Because we couldn't let anybody know what we'd
    been doing. I mean, we were absent without
    leave, in possession of alcohol and we'd stolen a
    canoe. What I didn't know was the officer on
    duty had witnessed this whole thing. Townsend

goes to the infirmary and is confronted with these charges and he admits everything. I didn't know that. I'm rudely awakened out of my sleep and hauled up before old Adjutant Perrault.

At attention, addressing the Adjutant Officer.

Sir! I've been in my bed all night. I really don't know what you're talking about, Sir.

PERRAULT:
Come on. Come on now, Bishop. We have the testimony of the officer on duty. We also have the full confession of your accomplice implicating you fully in this. Now, what is your story, Bishop?

BISHOP: *to the audience*
Well, I figured I was in too deep now to change my story.

To PERRAULT.

Sir, I still maintain. . . .

PERRAULT:
Bishop! I'm going to say the worst thing that I can say to a gentleman cadet. You are a liar, Bishop!

BISHOP is sobered briefly by the memory, but he quickly recovers.

BISHOP: *to the audience*

I got twenty-eight days restricted leave for that.
It's like house arrest. Then they caught me
cheating on my final exams. Well, I handed in
the crib notes with the exam paper! And that's
when they called me the worst student R.M.C.
ever had. They weren't going to tell me what my
punishment was until the next fall, so I could
stew about it all summer, but I knew what it
was going to be. Expulsion! With full honours!
But then the war broke out and I enlisted and
was made an officer. I mean, for me, it was the
lesser of two evils. But everyone else was very
keen on the whole thing. They were.

BISHOP AND PIANO PLAYER: *singing*

We were off to fight the Hun,
Though hardly anyone
Had ever seen a Hun,
Wouldn't know one if we saw one.
We were off to fight the Hun
And it looked like lots of fun,
Somehow it didn't seem like war
At all, at all, at all.
Somehow it didn't seem like war at all.

The PIANO PLAYER raps out a military
rhythm.

BISHOP: *to the audience*

October 1st, 1914, the First Contingent of the
Canadian Expeditionary Forces left for England.
I wasn't with them. I was in the hospital.
Thinking of Margaret. . . .

The PIANO PLAYER plays the appropriate
"Dear Margaret" music under the following speech.

24

As if writing a letter.

Dear...Dearest Margaret. I am in the hospital with pneumonia. I also have an allergy, but the doctors don't know what I am allergic to. Maybe it's horses. Maybe it's the Army. The hospital is nice, so I am in good spirits. Thinking of you constantly, I remain....

The PIANO PLAYER raps out a military rhythm once again.

To the audience.

March, 1915, the Second, Third, Fourth, Fifth and Sixth Contingents of the Canadian Expeditionary Forces left for England. I wasn't with them either. I was back in the hospital ...thinking of Margaret.

As if writing a letter.

Sweetheart. Please excuse my writing, as I have a badly sprained wrist. Yesterday, my horse reared up and fell over backwards on me. It was awful, I could have been killed. My head was completely buried in the mud. My nose is, of course, broken and quite swollen, and I can't see out of one eye. I have two broken ribs and am pretty badly bruised, but the doctor figures I'll be up and around by Monday. The hospital is nice, so I am in fine spirits. Thinking of you constantly, I remain....

The PIANO PLAYER raps out a military rhythm once again.

BISHOP: *to the audience*

June, 1915. The Seventh Contingent of the Canadian Expeditionary Forces left for England. I was with them. Now, this was aboard a cattle boat called the Caledonia, in Montreal. There was this big crowd came down to the pier to see us off. I mean, hundreds and hundreds of people, and for a while there, I felt like the whole thing was worth doing. It's pretty impressive when you look out there and you see several hundred people cheering and waving... at you. I mean, when you're from a small town, the numbers get to you. And you're looking out at them and they're looking back at you, and you think, "Boy, I must be doing something right!"

The PIANO PLAYER strikes up a "God Save the King."

And they play "God Save the King," and everybody is crying and waving and cheering, and the boat starts to pull out, and they start to yell like you've never heard anybody yell before. I mean, you feel good. You really do! And we're all praying, "Please God, don't let the fighting be over before I can get over there and take part...."

He becomes carried away and starts yelling.

"On the edge of destiny, you must test your strength!"

He is suddenly self-conscious

What the hell am I talking about?

26

The music changes from heroic to the monotonous roll of a ship.

BISHOP:

The good ship Caledonia soon changed it's name to the good ship Vomit. It was never meant to hold people. Even the horses didn't like it. Up, down, up, down. And they're siphoning brandy down our throats to keep us from puking our guts up on the deck. It was a big joke. Whenever anyone would puke, which was every minute or so, everyone would point to him and laugh like it was the funniest thing they had ever seen. I mean, puke swishing around on the deck, two inches deep, har, har, har! You couldn't sleep, even if it was calm, because every time you closed your eyes, you had a nightmare about being torpedoed.

He demonstrates a torpedo hitting the ship.

Every time I closed my eyes, I could see this torpedo coming up through the water, through the hull of the ship and...BOOM! And we were attacked, too, just off the coast of Ireland. I was scared shitless. All you could do was stand at the rail and watch the other ships get hit and go down. Bodies floating around like driftwood. But we made it through. The Good Ship Caledonia, latrine of the Atlantic, finally made it through to Portsmouth, full of dead horses and sick Canadians. When we got off, they thought we were a boat load of Balkan refugees.

BISHOP AND PIANO PLAYER: *singing*

> *We were off to fight the Hun,*
> *We would shoot him with a gun.*
> *Our medals would shine*
> *Like a sabre in the sun.*
> *We were off to fight the Hun*
> *And it looked like lots of fun,*
> *Somehow it didn't seem like war*
> *At all, at all, at all.*
> *Somehow it didn't seem like war at all.*

BISHOP: *to the audience*

A few days later, we marched into Shorncliffe
Military Camp, right on the Channel. You
know, on a clear night, you could see the
artillery flashes from France. I took it as a sign
of better things to come. . . . It wasn't.

> *As if writing a letter.*

Dearest Margaret. . . Shorncliffe Military Camp
is the worst yet! The cold wind brings two kinds
of weather. Either it rains or it doesn't. When it
rains, you've got mud like I've never seen
before. Your horse gets stuck in a foot and a
half of mud. You get off and you're knee deep.
The rain falls in sheets and you're wet to the
skin. You are never dry. Then the rain stops
and the ground dries out. What a relief, you
say? Then the wind gets the dust going and you
have dust storms for days. The sand is like
needles hitting you, and a lot of the men are
bleeding from the eyes. I don't know which is
worse, going blind or going crazy. The sand gets
in your food, your clothes, your tent, in
your. . . body orifices. A lot of the guys have

something called desert madness, which is really serious. As I write this letter, the sand is drifting across the page. Thinking of you constantly, I remain. . . .

To the audience.

Being buried alive in the mud. . . . I was seriously considering this proposition one day when a funny thing happened.

He demonstrates with a chair.

I got my horse stuck in the middle of the parade ground. The horse is up to its fetlocks; I'm up to my knees. Mud, sweat and horse shit from head to toe.

The music becomes ethereal and gentle.

Then, suddenly, out of the clouds comes this little single-seater scout. You know, this little fighter plane? It circles a couple of times. I guess the pilot had lost his way and was going to come down and ask for directions. He does this turn, then lands on an open space, like a dragonfly on a rock. The pilot jumps out. He's in this long sheepskin coat, helmet, goggles. . .warm and dry. He gets his directions, then jumps back into the machine, up in the air, with the mist blowing off him. All by himself. No superior officer, no horse, no sand, no mud. What a beautiful picture! I don't know how long I just stood there watching until he was long gone. Out of sight.

He breaks the mood abruptly.

30

BISHOP:
> I mean, this war was going on a lot longer than anyone expected. A lot more people were getting killed than anyone expected. Now I wasn't going to spend the rest of the war in the mud. And I sure as hell wasn't going to die in the mud.

> *The PIANO PLAYER strikes up a new tune.*
> *BISHOP drunkenly joins in.*

BISHOP AND PIANO PLAYER: *singing*
> *Thinking of December nights*
> *In the clear Canadian cold,*
> *Where the winter air don't smell bad,*
> *And the wind don't make you old.*
> *Where the rain don't wash your heart out,*
> *And the nights ain't filled with fear.*
> *Oh, those old familiar voices*
> *Whisper in my ears.*

Chorus

> *Oh, Canada,*
> *Sing a song for me.*
> *Sing one for your lonely son,*
> *So far across the sea.*

> *The piano continues with a popular dance tune of the period. BISHOP's reverie is interrupted by a Cockney OFFICER, who is also drunk, and who is slightly mad.*

OFFICER:
> You don't fancy the Cavalry then, eh?

BISHOP:
> What?!

OFFICER:

I say, you don't fancy the Cavalry then, eh? It's going to be worse at the front, mate. There, you got blokes shooting at you, right?...With machine guns.

He imitates a machine gun.

DakDakDakDakakaka. Har, har, har. It's a bloody shooting gallery. They still think they're fighting the Boer War! Cavalry charges against machine guns. DakDakDakak. Har, har! It's a bloody shooting gallery with you in the middle of it, mate.

BISHOP:

This is awful. Something's got to be done. Jeez, I was a casualty in training.

OFFICER:

Take a word of advice from me, mate. The only way out is up.

BISHOP:

Up?

OFFICER:

Up. Join the Royal Flying Corps. I did. I used to be in the Cavalry, but I joined the R.F.C. I like it. It's good clean work. Mind you, the bleeding machines barely stay in the air and the life expectancy of the new lads is about eleven days. But I like it. It's good clean work.

BISHOP:

> Just a minute. How can I get into the Royal
> Flying Corps? I'm Canadian. I'm cannon fodder.
> You practically have to own your own plane to
> get into the R.F.C.

OFFICER:

> Au contraire, mate. Au contraire. The upper
> classes are depressed by the present statistics, so
> they aren't joining with their usual alacrity.
> Now, anyone who wants to can get blown out of
> the air. Even Canadians.

BISHOP:

> Well, what do I have to do?

OFFICER:

> You go down to see them at the War Office,
> daft bunch of twits, but they're all right.
> Now . . . you act real eager, see? Like you want
> to be a pilot. You crave the excitement, any old
> rubbish like that. Then, they're not going to
> know what to ask, because they don't know a
> bleeding thing about it. So, they'll ask you
> whatever comes into their heads, which isn't
> much, then they'll say you can't be a pilot,
> you've got to be an observer.

BISHOP:

> What's an observer?

OFFICER:

> He's the fellow who goes along for the ride, you
> know? Looks about.

BISHOP:

> Ohhh. . . .

OFFICER:

So, you act real disappointed, like your Mum wanted you to be a pilot, and then, you get your transfer....

BISHOP:

Just a minute. So, I'm an observer. I'm the fellow that goes along for the ride, looks about. So what? How do I get to be a pilot?

OFFICER:

I don't know. Sooner or later, you just get to be a pilot. Plenty of vacancies these days. Check the casualty lists, wait for a bad one. You've got to go in by the back door, you know what I mean? Nobody gets to be a pilot right away, for Christ's sake. Especially not bleeding Canadians!

BISHOP: *to the audience*

Did you ever trust your future to a drunken conversation in a bar? Two days later, I went down to see them at the War Office.

The PIANO PLAYER plays some going to war music.

In the following scene, SIR HUGH CECIL interviews BISHOP at the War Office. He is getting on in years and the new technology of warfare has confused him deeply.

SIR HUGH:

So...you wish to transfer to the Royal Flying Corps? Am I right? Am I correct?

BISHOP:

Yes, Sir. I want to become a fighter pilot, Sir. It's what my mother always wanted, Sir.

SIR HUGH:

> Oh...I see. Well, the situation is this, Bishop.
> We need good men in the R.F.C., but they
> must have the correct...er...qualifications.
> Now, while the War Office has not yet
> ascertained what qualifications are indeed
> necessary to fly an...er...aeroplane, we must
> see to it that all candidates possess the necessary
> qualifications, should the War Office ever decide
> what those qualifications are. Do you
> understand, Bishop?

BISHOP:

> Perfectly, Sir.

SIR HUGH:

> That's very good. Jolly Good. More than I can
> say. Well, shall we begin then?

BISHOP:

> Ready when you are, Sir.

SIR HUGH:

> That's good, shows keenness, you see....And
> good luck, Bishop.

> *To himself.*

What on earth shall I ask him?

> *There is a long pause while he collects his
> thoughts.*

Do you ski?

BISHOP:

> Ski, sir?

SIR HUGH:
     Yes...do you ski?

BISHOP: *to the audience*
     Here was an Englishman asking a Canadian
     whether or not he skied. Now, if the Canadian
     said he didn't ski, the Englishman might find
     that somewhat suspicious.

     To SIR HUGH.

     Ski? Yes, Sir.

     To the audience.

     Never skied in my life.

SIR HUGH:
     Fine, well done...thought you might.

     Pause.

     Do you ride a horse?

BISHOP:
     I'm an officer in the Cavalry, Sir.

SIR HUGH:
     Doesn't necessarily follow, but we'll put down
     that you ride, shall we?

     Pause.

     What about sports, Bishop? Run, jump, throw
     the ball? Play the game, eh? What?

BISHOP:
>Sports, Sir? All sports.

SIR HUGH:
>I see. Well done, Bishop. I'm most impressed.

BISHOP:
>Does this mean I can become a fighter pilot, Sir?

SIR HUGH:
>Who knows, Bishop? Who knows? All full up with fighter pilots at the moment, I'm afraid. Take six months, a year to get in. Terribly sorry. Nothing I can do, old man.

BISHOP:
>I see, Sir.

SIR HUGH:
>However! We have an immediate need for observers. You know, the fellow who goes along for the ride, looks about. What do you say, Bishop?

BISHOP: *to the audience*
>I thought about it. I wanted to be a pilot. I couldn't. So, in the fall of 1915, I joined the Twenty-First Squadron as an observer. That's what they were using planes for at that time. Observation. You could take pictures of enemy troop formations, direct artillery fire, stuff like that. It seemed like nice quiet work at the time and I was really good at the aerial photography. I've got these great eyes, remember? And to fly! You're in this old Farnham trainer, sounds like a tractor. It coughs, wheezes, chugs it's way up to one thousand feet. You're in a kite with a motor

that can barely get off the ground. But even so, you're in the air. . . . You're not on the ground. . . . You're above everything.

The PIANO PLAYER plays some mess hall music.

It was a different world up there. A different war and a different breed of men fighting that war. . . . Flyers! During training, we heard all the stories. If you went down behind enemy lines and were killed, they'd come over, the Germans, that is . . . they'd come over under a flag of truce and drop a photograph of your grave. Nice. If you were taken prisoner, it was the champagne razzle in the mess. Talking and drinking all night. It was a different war they were fighting up there. And from where I stood, it looked pretty darn good.

PIANO PLAYER:
Can you be a bit more specific, please?

BISHOP and the PIANO PLAYER sing a song of champagne and vermouth.

BISHOP AND PIANO PLAYER: *singing*
I see two planes in the air,
A fight that's fair and square,
With dips and loops and rolls
That would scare you (I'm scared already).
We will force the German down
And arrest him on the ground,
A patriotic lad from Bavaria (Poor bloody sod).

But he'll surrender willingly
And salute our chivalry,
For this war is not of our creation.

But before it's prison camp
And a bed that's cold and damp,
We'll all have a little celebration.

Chorus

Oh, we'll toast our youth
On champagne and vermouth,
For all of us know what it's like to fly.
Oh, the fortunes of war
Can't erase esprit de corps
And we'll all of us be friends
'Til we die.

PIANO PLAYER:
Can you go on a bit, please?

BISHOP AND PIANO PLAYER: *singing*
Oh, we'll drink the night away,
And when the Bosch is led away,
We'll load him down with cigarettes and wine.
We'll drink a final toast goodbye,
But for the grace of God go I,
And we'll vow that we'll be friends (Cheers — ping)
Another time.

Chorus

Oh, we'll toast our youth
On champagne and vermouth,
For all of us know what it's like to fly.
Oh, the fortunes of war
Can't erase esprit de corps
And we'll all of us be friends
'Til we die.

BISHOP:

You want chivalry? You want gallantry? You
want nice guys? That's your flyer. And Jeez, I
was going to be one! January 1st, 1916, I
crossed the channel to France as a flyer. Well,
an observer anyway. That's when I found out
that Twenty-First Squadron was known as the
"suicide squadron." I mean, that awful nickname
used to pray on my mind, you know? And the
Archies? The anti-aircraft guns? Not tonight,
Archibald! I mean, you're tooling around
over the line, doing your observation work, a
sitting duck, when suddenly you are surrounded
by these little black puffs of smoke.
Then . . . wham-whizz! Shrapnel whizzes all
around you. I was hit on the head by a piece of
flak, just a bruise, but a couple of inches lower
and I would have been killed. And we were all
scared stiff of this new German machine, the
Fokker. It had this interrupter gear, so the pilot
could shoot straight at you through the propeller
without actually shooting the propeller off. All
he had to do was aim his plane at you! And
casualties? Lots and lots and lots of casualties. It
was a grim situation. But we didn't know how
grim it could get until we saw the RE-7 . . . the
Reconnaissance Experimental Number
Seven. Our new plane. What you saw was
this mound of cables and wires, with a thousand
pounds of equipment hanging off it. Four
machine guns, a five hundred pound bomb, for
God's sake. Reconnaissance equipment,
cameras. . . . Roger Neville (that's my pilot), he
and I are ordered into the thing to take it up. Of
course, it doesn't get off the ground. Anyone
could see that. We thought, fine, good riddance.
But the officers go into a huddle.

BISHOP: *imitating the Officers*

Mmmmum? What do you think we should do? Take the bomb off? Take the bomb off!

As himself.

So we take the bomb off and try it again. This time, the thing sort of flops down the runway like a crippled duck. Finally, by taking everything off but one machine gun, the thing sort of flopped itself into the air and chugged along. It was a pig! We were all scared stiff of it. So they put us on active duty...as *bombers*! They gave us two bombs each, told us to fly over Hunland and drop them on somebody. But in order to accommodate for the weight of the bombs, they took our machine guns away!

As if writing a letter.

Dearest Margaret. We are dropping bombs on the enemy from unarmed machines. It is exciting work. It's hard to keep your confidence in a war when you don't have a gun. Somehow we get back in one piece and we start joking around and inspecting the machine for bullet and shrapnel damage. You're so thankful not to be dead. Then I go back to the barracks and lie down. A kind of terrible loneliness comes over me. It's like waiting for the firing squad. It makes you want to cry, you feel so frightened and so alone. I think all of us who aren't dead think these things. Thinking of you constantly, I remain....

PIANO PLAYER: *singing*

> *Nobody shoots no one in Canada,*
> *At least nobody they don't know.*
> *Nobody shoots no one in Canada,*
> *Last battle was a long, long time ago.*
>
> *Nobody picks no fights in Canada,*
> *Not with nobody they ain't met.*
> *Nobody starts no wars in Canada,*
> *Folks tend to work for what they get.*
>
> *Take me under*
> *That big blue sky,*
> *Where the deer and the black bear play.*
> *May not be heaven,*
> *But heaven knows we try,*
> *Wish I was in Canada today.*
>
> *Nobody drop no bombs on Canada,*
> *Wouldn't want to send no one to hell.*
> *Nobody start no wars on Canada,*
> *Where folks tend to wish each other well.*

The music continues as BISHOP speaks.

BISHOP:

Of course in this situation, it wasn't too long
before the accidents started happening again. It's
kind of spooky, but I think being accident prone
actually saved my life. I'm driving a truck load
of parts a couple of miles from the aerodrome
and I run into another truck. I'm inspecting the
undercarriage of my machine when a cable
snaps and hits me on the head. I was
unconscious for two days. . . . I had a tooth
pulled, it got infected and I was in the hospital
for two weeks. . . . Then Roger does this really

bad landing. I hit my knee on a metal brace inside the plane so hard I could barely walk. . . . Then I got three weeks leave in London. None too soon. On the boat going back to England, we all got into the champagne and cognac pretty heavy, and, by the time we arrived, we were all pretty tight and this game developed to see who would actually be the first guy to touch foot on English soil. I'm leading the race down the gangplank. I trip and fall! Everyone else falls on top of me, right on the knee I hurt in the crash! Gawd, the pain was awful! But I was damned if I'd spend my leave in the hospital, so I'd just pour down the brandy until the thing was pretty well numb. I had a hell of a time! If the pain got to me in the night and I couldn't sleep, I'd just pour down the brandy. But around my last day of leave, I started thinking about the bombing runs, the Archies, the Fokkers, and I thought, Jeez, maybe I better have someone look at this knee. The doctor found I had a cracked kneecap, which meant I'd be in the hospital for a couple of weeks. They also found I had a badly strained heart, which meant I would be in the hospital for an indefinite period. As far as I was concerned, I was out of the war.

BISHOP AND PIANO PLAYER: *singing*
> *Take me under*
> *That big blue sky,*
> *Where the deer and the black bear play.*
> *It may not be heaven,*
> *But heaven knows we try,*
> *Wish I was in Canada today.*

I'm dreaming of the trees in Canada,
Northern Lights are dancing in my head.
If I die, then let me die in Canada,
Where there's a chance I'll die in bed.

BISHOP:

The hospital is nice. People don't shoot at you and people don't drop things on you. I thought it would be a nice place to spend the rest of the war. I went to sleep for three days.

Distorted marching music is heard.

I had this nightmare. A terrible dream. I am in the lobby of the Grand Hotel in London. The band is playing military music and the lobby is full of English and German officers. They're dancing together and their medals jingle like sleighbells in the snow. The sound is deafening. I've got to get out of there. I start to run, but my knee gives out underneath me. As I get up, I get kicked in the stomach by a Prussian boot. As I turn to run, I get kicked in the rear by an English boot. Then I turn around and all the officers have formed a chorus line, like the Follies, and they are heading for me, kicking. I scream as a hundred black boots kick me high in the air, as I turn over and over, shouting, "Help me! Help me! They are trying to kill me!"

He wakes up abruptly.

LADY ST. HELIER:

My goodness, Bishop, you'll not get any rest screaming at the top of your lungs like that.

BISHOP: *to the audience*
> In front of me was a face I'd never seen before.
> Very old, female, with long white hair pulled
> back tightly in a bun, exposing two of the largest
> ears I had ever seen.

LADY ST. HELIER:
> You'd be the son of Will Bishop of Owen Sound,
> Canada, would you not? Of course you are, the
> resemblance is quite startling. Your father was a
> loyal supporter of a very dear friend of mine, Sir
> Wilfred Laurier. It was in that connection I met
> your father in Ottawa.

> *She zeros in on BISHOP.*

> A gaping mouth is most impolite, Bishop. No, I
> am not clairvoyant. I am Lady St. Helier.
> Reform alderman, poetess, friend of Churchill,
> and the women who shall save your life.

BISHOP: *speechless*
> Ahh...oh...mmmm. Ahhh....

LADY ST. HELIER:
> Enough of this gay banter, Bishop. Time runs
> apace and my life is not without its limits. You
> have been making rather a mess of it, haven't
> you? You are a rude young man behaving like
> cannon fodder. Perfectly acceptable
> characteristics in a Canadian, but you are
> different. You are a gifted Canadian and that
> gift belongs to a much older and deeper
> tradition than Canada can ever hope to provide.
> Quite against your own wishes, you will be
> released from this wretched hospital in two
> weeks' time. Promptly, at three o'clock on that
> afternoon, you will present yourself before my

door at Portland Place, dressed for tea and in a positive frame of mind. Do I make myself clear? Good. Please be punctual, Mr. Bishop.

BISHOP: *to the audience*
Well, Jeez, that old girl must have known something I didn't, because, two weeks later, I'm released from hospital. Promptly, at three o'clock, I find myself in front of her door at Portland Place, in my best uniform, shining my shoes on my pants. The door is opened by the biggest butler I have ever seen.

He looks up and speaks to the butler.

Hi!

The butler looks down at him with distaste, turns away and calls to LADY ST. HELIER.

CEDRIC: *calling*
Madam, the Canadian is here. Shall I show him in?

LADY ST. HELIER: *from a distance*
Yes, Cedric, please. Show him in.

CEDRIC: *turning his back to BISHOP*
Get in!

BISHOP: *to the audience*
I'm shown into the largest room I've ever seen. I mean, a fireplace eight feet wide and a staircase that must have had a hundred steps in it. I'm not used to dealing with nobility. Servants, grand ballrooms, pheasant hunting on the heath, fifty-year-old brandy over billiards, breakfast in bed...shit, what a life!

CEDRIC:
> Madam is in the study. Get in!

BISHOP:
> The study. Books, books...more books than I'll
> ever read. Persian rug. Tiger's head over the
> mantle. African spears in the corner. "Rule
> Britannia, Britannia rules the...." I stood at the
> door. I was on edge. Out of my element. Lady
> St. Helier was sitting at this little writing desk,
> writing.

LADY ST. HELIER:
> Very punctual, Bishop. Please sit down.

BISHOP:
> I sat in this chair that was all carved lions. One
> of the lions stuck in my back.

CEDRIC:
> Would our visitor from Canada care for tea,
> madam?

LADY ST. HELIER:
> Would you care for something to drink, Bishop?

BISHOP:
> Tea? Ahhh, yeah....Tea would be fine.

LADY ST. HELIER:
> A tea for Bishop, Cedric. And I'll have a gin.

CEDRIC:
> Lemon?

BISHOP: *disappointed*
> Gin! I wonder if I could change....No, no. Tea
> will be fine.

BISHOP: *to the audience*
Tea was served. I sip my tea. Lady St. Helier
sips her gin. And Cedric loomed over me, afraid
I was going to drool on the carpet or something.
Lady St. Helier stared at me through her thick
spectacles. Suddenly, her ears twitched, like she
was honing in on something.

LADY ST. HELIER:
I have written a poem in your honour, Bishop. I
can but hope that your rustic mind will
appreciate its significance.

She signals to the PIANO PLAYER.

Cedric!

LADY ST. HELIER: *spoken to music*
You're a typical Canadian,
You're modesty itself,
And you really wouldn't want to hurt a flea.
But you're just about to go
The way of the buffalo.
You'd do well to take this good advice from me.

I'm awfully sick and tired
Being constantly required
To stand by and watch Canadians make the best of it,
For the Colonial mentality
Defies all rationality.
You seem to go to lengths to make a mess of it.

Why don't you grow up,
Before I throw up?
Do you expect somebody else to do it for you?
Before you're dead out,
Get the lead out
And seize what little life still lies before you.

Do you really expect Empire
To settle back, retire,
And say, "Colonials, go on your merry way"?
I'm very tired of your whining
And your infantile maligning.
Your own weakness simply won't be whined away.

So don't be so naïve,
And take that heart off your sleeve,
For a fool and his life will soon be parted.
War's a fact of life today
And it will not be wished away.
Forget that fact and you'll be dead before you've started.

So, Bishop, grow up,
Before I throw up.
You're worst enemy is yourself, as you well know.
Before you're dead out,
Get the lead out.
You have your own naïvité to overthrow.

LADY ST. HELIER: *to the PIANO PLAYER*
Thank you, Cedric.

To BISHOP.

Do I make myself clear, Bishop? You will cease
this mediocrity your record only too clearly
reveals. You will become the pilot you wished to
be but were lamentably content to settle for less.
Now this will take time, for you must recover
the health you have so seriously undermined. To
that end, you will remain here, a lodger at
Portland Place, top of the stairs, third floor,
seventh room on the left. Cedric, be kind to
Bishop and ignore his bad manners. For
cultivation exacts its price. The loss of a
certain...vitality. Beneath this rude Canadian

exterior, there is a power that you will never know. Properly harnessed, that power will win wars for you. Churchill knows it and I know it too. Good day, Bishop.

BISHOP: *to the audience*
Now there are one or two Canadians who would have taken offence at that. Not me. Staying at Portland Place, I found out some things right away. For example, life goes much smoother when you've got influence. Take this pilot business, for example. Lady St. Helier was on the phone to Churchill himself, and, the next day, I was called down to the War Office. The atmosphere was much different.

Going to war music is heard once again.

SIR HUGH:
Bishop, my boy. Good to see you, good to see you. Well, well, well, your mother's wish is finally going to come true.

BISHOP:
Really, Sir?

SIR HUGH:
Yes, yes. You are going to become a pilot. No problem, pas de problème. Medical examination in two days time, then report for training.

BISHOP: *to the audience*
Medical examination! What about my weak heart? What about the fact that three weeks ago I was on the verge of a medical discharge?

DOCTOR: *addressing BISHOP, but seldom ever looking up from his desk.* Strip to the waist, Bishop. Hmnmnmnm? Stick out your tongue and say ninety-nine. . . .Good. . . .Cough twice. . . . That's good, too. . . .Turn around ten times . . . .Eight, nine, ten. . . .Attention! Still on your feet, Bishop? You're fit as a fiddle and ready to fly!

BISHOP: *singing*
Gonna fly. . .
Gonna fly so high,
Like a bird in the sky,
With the wind in my hair,
And the sun burning in my eyes.
Flying Canadian,
Machine gun in my hand,
First Hun I see is the first Hun to die.

Gonna fly. . .
In my machine,
Gonna shoot so clean,
Gonna hear them scream
When I hit them between the eyes.
Flying Canadian,
Machine gun in my hand,
First Hun I see is the first Hun to die.

Chorus

Flying. . .
What have I been waiting for?
What a way to fight a war!
Flying Canadian,
Machine gun in my hand,
First Hun I see is the first Hun to die.

Gonna fly. . .
Gonna shoot them down
'Til they hit the ground
And they burn with the sound
Of bacon on the fry.
Flying Canadian,
Machine gun in my hand,
First Hun I see is the first Hun to die.

Chorus

Flying. . .
What have I been waiting for?
What a way to fight a war!
Flying Canadian,
Machine gun in my hand,
First Hun I see is the first Hun to die.

> *The song ends abruptly.*

BISHOP:
> I'll never forget my first solo flight. Lonely?
> Jeeezus! You're sitting at the controls all by
> yourself, trying to remember what they're all for.
> Everyone has stopped doing what they're doing
> to watch you. An ambulance is parked at the
> edge of the field with the engines running. You
> know why. You also know that there's a surgical
> team in the hospital, just ready to rip.

> *The PIANO PLAYER calls out the following.*
> *BISHOP repeats after him.*

PIANO PLAYER:
> Switch off.

BISHOP:
> Switch off.

PIANO PLAYER:
>Petrol on.

BISHOP:
>Petrol on.

PIANO PLAYER:
>Suck in.

BISHOP:
>Suck in.

PIANO PLAYER:
>Switch on.

BISHOP:
>Switch on.

PIANO PLAYER:
>Contact!

BISHOP:
>Contact!

>>*During the above, BISHOP does all the sound effects vocally, much as a small boy would do during such a demonstration.*

The propellor is given a sharp swing over and the engine starts with a roar. . .coughs twice, but soon starts hitting on all cylinders. You signal for them to take away the chocks. Then you start bouncing across the field under your own power and head her up into the wind.

>*He checks the equipment.*

Rudder.

Click, click.

Elevator.

Click, click.

Ailerons.

Click, click.

Heart.

Boom-boom! Boom-boom!

I open the throttle all the way. . .and you're off!
Pull back on the stick, easy, easy.

He demonstrates the plane bumping along, then rising up into the air.

Once I was in the air, I felt a lot better. In fact, I felt like a king! Mind you, I wasn't fooling around. I'm flying straight as I can, climbing steadily. All alone! What a feeling!

He looks about.

I've got to turn. I execute a gentle turn, skidding like crazy, but what the hell. I try another turn. This time, I bank it a little more. Too much. Too much!. . .All in all, I'm having a hell of a time up there until I remember I have to land. . . .What do I do now? Keep your head, that's what you do. Pull back on the throttle.

The engine coughs.

Too much! I put the nose down into a steep dive. Too steep. Bring it up again, down again, up, down . . . and in a series of steps, kind of descend to the earth. Then I execute everything I remember I have to do to make a perfect landing. Forty feet off the ground! I put the nose down again and do another perfect landing. This time, I'm only eight feet off the ground, but now I don't have room left to do another nose down manoeuvre. The rumpty takes things into her own hands and just pancakes the rest of the way to the ground. First solo flight! Greatest day in a man's life!

PIANO PLAYER AND BISHOP: *singing*
Flying . . .
What have I been waiting for?
What a way to fight a war!
Flying Canadian,
Machine gun in my hand,
First Hun I see is the first Hun to die,
First Hun I see is the first Hun to die.

BISHOP:
In the early part of 1916, I was posted back to France as a fighter pilot. Sixtieth Squadron, Third British Brigade. I worked like a Trojan for these wings and I just about lost them before I really began. I was returning from my first O.P., Operational Patrol, and I crashed my Nieuport on landing. I wasn't hurt, but the aircraft was pretty well pranged, and that was bad because General John Higgins, the Brigade Commander, saw me do it. Well, he couldn't help but see me do it. I just about crashed at his feet!

HIGGINS:

I watched you yesterday, Bishop. You destroyed a machine. A very expensive, a very nice machine. Doing a simple landing on a clear day. That machine was more valuable than you'll ever be, buck-o.

BISHOP:

Sir, there was a gust of wind from the hangar. I mean, ask Major Scott, our patrol leader. It could have happened to anyone.

HIGGINS:

I was on the field, Bishop.

BISHOP:

Yes, Sir.

HIGGINS:

There was no wind.

BISHOP:

No wind? Yes, Sir.

HIGGINS:

I have your record here on my desk, Bishop, and it isn't a very impressive document. On the positive side, you were wounded. And you score well in target practice, although you have never actually fired upon the enemy. The list of your negative accomplishments is longer, isn't it, much longer? Conduct unbecoming an officer. Breaches of discipline. A lot of silly accidents, suspicious accidents, if I might say so. A trail of wrecked machinery in your wake. You are a terrible pilot, Bishop. In short, you are a liability to the R.F.C. and I wish to God you were back in Canada where you belong, or failing that, digging a trench in some unstrategic valley. In short, you are finished, Bishop, finished. When your replacement arrives, he will replace you. That is all.

BISHOP:

That was the lowest point of my career. Then came March 25, 1917.

The following is performed on microphone with BISHOP creating the sound effects. The PIANO PLAYER joins him. The mike should be used as a joy stick and the aggression implied in the story should be transferred to the microphone.

March 25, 1917. Four Nieuport scouts in diamond formation climb to nine thousand feet crossing the line somewhere between Arras and St. Léger. Our patrol is to crisscross the lines noting Heinie's positions and troop movements.

The sound of airplane engine is heard.

RRrrr. I'm the last man in that patrol, tough place to be because, if you fall too far behind, the headhunters are waiting for you. It starts out cloudy, then suddenly clears up. We fly for half an hour and don't see anything, just miles and miles of nothing. RRrrr. Suddenly, I see four specks above and behind us. A perfect place for an enemy attack. I watch as the specks get larger. I can make out the black crosses on them. Huns! It's hard to believe that they are real, alive and hostile. I want to circle around and have a better look at them. Albatross "V" strutters, beautiful, with their swept back planes, powerful and quick. RRrrrr. We keep on flying straight. Jack Scott, our leader, either hasn't seen them or he wants them to think that he hasn't seen them. They are getting closer and closer. We keep on flying straight. They are two hundred yards behind us, getting closer and closer. Suddenly, RRrrr! Jack Scott opens out into a sharp climbing turn to get above and behind them. The rest of us follow. Rrrrr! RRrrr! RRrrrr! I'm slower than the rest and come out about forty yards behind. In front of me, a dogfight is happening, right in front of my very eyes. Real pandemonium, planes turning every which way. RRRrr! Machine gun fire. Suddenly, Jack Scott sweeps below me with an Albatross on his tail raking his fuselage and wing tips with gunfire! For a moment, I'm just frozen there, not knowing what to do, my whole body just shaking! Then I throw the stick forward and dive on the Hun. I keep him in my Aldis sight 'til he completely fills the lens. AKAKAkak! What a feeling, as he flips over on his back and falls out of control! But wait, wait. . . . Grid Caldwell warned me about this. He's not out of control, he's faking it. He's going to level out at two thousand feet and escape. Bastard! I dive after him with my engine full on. Sure enough, when he comes out of it, I'm right there. AKAkakaka! Again, my tracers smash into his machine. Gawd, I've got to be hitting him! He flips over on his back and is gone again. This time, I stay right with him. EEEeeeeee! The wires on my machine howl in protest. Nieuports have had their wings come off at 150 miles per hour. I must be doing 180. I just don't give a shit! I keep firing into the tumbling Hun. AKAKaka! He just crashes into the earth and explodes in flames. BAA-WHOOSH! I pull back on the stick, level out, screaming at the top of my lungs, I win, I WIN, I WIN!

The sound of wind is heard — no engine, no nothing.

Jeezus, my engine's stopped! It must have filled with oil on the dive. I try every trick in the book to get it going again. Nothing. Oh God, I'm going to go in! Down, down.

The sound of gunfire is heard.

Gunfire! I must still be over Hunland. Just my luck to do something right and end up being taken a prisoner. Lower and lower. I pick out what seems to be a level patch in the rough terrain and I put her down.

The sound of a bouncing crash is heard.

I got out of the plane into what must have been a shell hole. I took my Very Lite pistol with me. I wasn't exactly sure what I was going to do with it.

TOMMY: *in a "Canadian" accent*
Well...you're just in time for a cup of tea, lad.

BISHOP: *surprised*
ARrghgh...you spoke English! Hey, look, where am I?

TOMMY:

You're at the corner of Portage and Main in downtown Winnipeg. You want to keep down, lad. Heinie is sitting right over there. Well, goll, that was a nice bit of flying you did there! Yep, you're a hundred yards our side of the line.

BISHOP:

OOhhh, look...can you do me a favour? I'd like to try and get the plane up again.

TOMMY:

Not tonight, lad, nope....You're going to have to take the Montcalm Suite here at the Chateau.

BISHOP:

I spent the night in the trench in six inches of water! The soldiers seemed to be able to sleep. I couldn't.

The sound of shelling gets progressively louder.

Next morning at first light, I crawled out to see how my plane was. Miraculously, it hadn't been hit. And that's when I got my first real look at "No Man's Land." Jeezus, what a mess! Hardly a tree left standing. And the smell! It was hard to believe you were still on earth. I saw a couple of Tommys sleeping in a trench nearby.

He goes over to the Tommys.

Hey, you guys, I wonder if you could give me a hand with...?

He takes a closer look. The Tommys aren't asleep. He backs off with a shudder.

*The PIANO PLAYER sings and BILLY
BISHOP joins him.*

BISHOP AND PIANO PLAYER: *singing*
*Oh, the bloody earth is littered
With the fighters and the quitters.
Oh, what could be more bitter
Than a nameless death below.
See the trenches, long and winding,
See the battle slowly grinding,
Don't you wonder how good men can live so low.*

*Up above, the clouds are turning,
Up above, the sun is burning,
You can hear those soldiers yearning:
"Oh, if only I could fly!"
From the burning sun, I'll sight you,
In the burning sun, I'll fight you.
Oh, let us dance together in the sky.*

Chorus

*In the sky,
In the sky,
Just you and I up there together,
Who knows why?
One the hunter, one the hunted;
A life to live a death confronted.
Oh, let us dance together in the sky.*

*And for you, the bell is ringing,
And for you, the bullets stinging.
My Lewis gun is singing:
"Oh, my friend, it's you or I."
And I'll watch your last returning
To the earth, the fires burning.
Look up and you will see me wave goodbye.*

Chorus

In the sky,
In the sky,
Just you and I up there together,
Who knows why?
One the hunter, one the hunted;
A life to live, a death confronted.
Oh, let us dance together in the sky.

Act Two

*The lights come up, as in Act One, with the
PIANO PLAYER and BILLY BISHOP at the
piano.*

BISHOP AND PIANO PLAYER: *singing*
> *Oh, the bold Aviator lay dying,*
> *As 'neath the wreckage he lay, (he lay),*
> *To the sobbing mechanics beside him,*
> *These last parting words he did say:*
>
> *Two valves you'll find in my stomach,*
> *Three sparkplugs are safe in my lung, (my lung).*
> *The prop is in splinters inside me,*
> *To my fingers, the joystick has clung.*
>
> *Then get you six brandies and soda,*
> *And lay them all out in a row, (a row),*
> *And get you six other good airmen,*
> *To drink to this pilot below.*

Take the cylinders out of my kidneys,
The connecting rod out of my brain, (my brain),
From the small of my back take the crankshaft,
And assemble the engine again!

> *The music changes to a theme reminiscent of a*
> *French café. Time has gone by and BISHOP has*
> *changed.*

BISHOP:
> Survival. That's the important thing. And the
> only way to learn survival is to survive. Success
> depends on accuracy and surprise. How well
> you shoot, how you get into the fight and how
> well you fly. In *that* order. I can't fly worth shit
> compared to someone like Barker or Ball, but I
> don't care. If I get a kill, it's usually in the first
> few seconds of the fight. Any longer than that
> and you might as well get the hell out. You've
> got to be good enough to get him in the first few
> bursts, so practice your shooting as much as you
> can. After patrols, between patrols, on your day
> off. If I get a clear shot at a guy, he's dead. You
> ever heard of "flamers"? That's when you bounce
> a machine and it just bursts into flames. Now, I
> don't want to sound bloodthirsty or anything,
> but when that happens, it is very satisfying. But
> it's almost always pure luck. You hit a gas line
> or something like that. If you want the machine
> to go down every time, you aim for one thing:
> the man. I always go for the man.

> *The music stops. The PIANO PLAYER becomes*
> *a French announcer.*

ANNOUNCER:

> Ladies and Gentlemen...Madames et
> Messieurs...Charlie's Bar, Amiens, proudly
> presents: The Lovely Hélène!

BISHOP: *as the Lovely Hélène, singing*
> *Johnny was a Christian,*
> *He was humble and humane.*
> *His conscience was clear,*
> *And his soul without a stain.*
> *He was contemplating heaven,*
> *When the wings fell off his plane.*
> *And he never got out alive,*
> *He didn't survive.*
>
> *George was patriotic,*
> *His country he adored.*
> *He was the first to volunteer,*
> *When his land took up the sword,*
> *And a half a dozen medals*
> *Were his posthumous reward.*
> *And he never got out alive,*
> *He didn't survive.*
>
> Chorus
>
> *So when you fight, stay as calm as the ocean,*
> *And watch what's going on behind your shoulder.*
> *Remember, war's not the place for deep emotion,*
> *And maybe you'll get a little older.*

BISHOP: *as himself*
> Come into a fight with an advantage: height,
> speed, surprise. Come at him out of the sun,
> he'll never see you. Get on his tail, his blind
> spot, so you can shoot him without too much
> risk to yourself. Generally, patrols don't watch
> behind them as much, so sneak up on the last

man. He'll never know what hit him. Then you get out in the confusion. Hunt them. Like Hell's Handmaiden. If it's one on one, you come at the bugger, head on, guns blazing. He chickens out and you get him as he comes across your sights. If you both veer the same way, you're dead, so it's tricky. You have to keep your nerve.

BISHOP: *as the Lovely Hélène, singing*
    Geoffrey made a virtue
    Out of cowardice and fear.
    He was the first to go on sick leave,
    And the last to volunteer.
    He was running from a fight,
    When they attacked him from the rear.
    And he never got out alive, (no),
    He didn't survive.

BISHOP: *as himself*
Another thing is your mental attitude. It's not like the infantry where a bunch of guys work themselves up into a screaming rage and tear off over the top, yelling and waving their bayonets. It's not like that. You're part of a machine, so you have to stay very calm and cold. You and your machine work together to bring the other fellow down. You get so you don't feel anything after a while...until the moment you start firing, and then that old dry throat, heartthrobbing thrill comes back. It's a great feeling!

BISHOP: *as the Lovely Hélène, singing*
    Jimmy hated Germans
    With a passion cold and deep.
    He cursed them when he saw them,
    He cursed them in his sleep.

71

He was cursing when his plane went down
And landed in a heap.
And he never got out alive, (no),
He didn't survive.

Chorus

So when you fight, stay as calm as the ocean,
And watch what's going on behind your shoulder.
Remember, war is not the place for deep emotion,
And maybe you'll get a little older.

BISHOP:

Bloody April? We lost just about everyone I started with. Knowles, Hall, Williams, Townsend, Chapman. Steadman, shot down the day he joined the squadron. You see, the Hun has better machines and some of their pilots are very good. But practice makes perfect, if you can stay alive long enough to practice. But it gets easier and easier to stay alive because hardly anyone else has the same experience as you. Oh yeah, another thing. You take your fun where you can find it.

The music and mood change.

He has noticed the Lovely Hélène. She has noticed him. They meet outside. Without a word, she signals him to follow. Silently, they walk down an alley, through an archway, and up a darkened stairway. They are in her room. He closes the door. He watches her light a candle. She turns to him and says: "I should not be doing this. My lover is a Colonel at the front. But you are so beautiful and so, so young." An hour later, they kiss in the darkened doorway.

She says: "If you see me, you do not know me." She's gone. He meets his friends who have all enjoyed the same good luck. It's late, they've missed the last bus to the aerodrome. Arm in arm, they walk in the moonlight, silently sharing a flask of brandy, breathing in that warm spring air. As they approach Filescamp, they begin to sing, loudly: "Mademoiselle from Armentières, parlez-vous. Mademoiselle from Armentières, parlez-vous"...as if to leave behind the feelings they have had that night. In an hour, they will be on patrol. They go to bed. They sleep.

There is an abrupt change of mood. BISHOP is flying and shooting once again.

As if writing a letter.

Dearest Margaret. It is the merry month of May, and today, I sent another merry Hun to his merry death. I'm not sure you'd appreciate the bloodthirsty streak that has come over me in the past months. How I hate the Hun. He has killed so many of my friends. I enjoy killing him now. I go up as much as I can, even on my day off. My score is getting higher and higher because I like it. Yesterday, I had a narrow escape. A bullet came through the windshield and creased my helmet. But a miss is as good as a mile and if I am for it, I am for it. But I do not believe I am for it. My superiors are pleased. Not only have I been made Captain, they are recommending me for the Military Cross. Thinking of you constantly, I remain. . . .

BISHOP AND PIANO PLAYER: *singing*
> *You may think you've something special*
> *That will get you through this war,*
> *But the odds aren't in your favour,*
> *That's a fact you can't ignore.*
> *The chances are, the man will come*
> *A-knocking at your door.*
> *And you'll never get out alive,*
> *And you won't survive.*

Chorus

> *So when you fight, stay as calm as the ocean,*
> *And watch what's going on behind your shoulder.*
> *Remember, war's not the place for deep emotion,*
> *And maybe you'll get a little older.*

The music stops. There is a blackout.

BISHOP talks to ALBERT BALL.

BISHOP:
Albert Ball, Britain's highest scoring pilot, sat before me. His black eyes gleamed at me, very pale, very intense. Back home, we would have said he had eyes like two pissholes in the snow. But that's not very romantic. And Albert Ball was romantic, if anybody was.

BALL:
Compatriots in Glory! Oh, Bishop, I have an absolutely ripping idea. I want you to try and picture this. Two pilots cross the line in the dim, early dawn. It is dark, a slight fog. They fly straight for the German aerodrome at Douai, ghosts in the night. The Hun, unsuspecting, sleeps cosily in his lair. The sentries are sleeping. Perhaps the Baron von Richthofen

74

himself is there, sleeping, dreaming of eagles and...wienerschnitzel. It is the moment of silence, just before dawn. Suddenly, he is awakened from his sleep by the sound of machine gun fire. He rushes to his window to see four, maybe five, of his best machines in flames. He watches as the frantic pilots try to take off and one by one are shot down. The two unknown raiders strike a devastating blow. Bishop, you and I are those two unknown raiders.

BISHOP:
Jeez, I like it. It's a good plan. How do we get out?

BALL:
Get out?

BISHOP:
Yeah. Get out? You know, escape!

BALL:
I don't think you get the picture, Bishop. It's a grand gesture. Getting out has nothing to do with it.

BISHOP:
Oh! Well, it's a good plan. It's got a few holes I'd like to see plugged. I'd like to think about it.

BALL:
All right, Bishop, you think about it. But remember this: Compatriots in Glory!

BISHOP:
Quite a fellow.

He turns to the audience and announces.

"The Dying of Albert Ball."

The following is performed like a Robert Service poem.

BISHOP:
> *He was only eighteen*
> *When he downed his first machine,*
> *And any chance of living through this war was small;*
> *He was nineteen when I met him,*
> *And I never will forget him,*
> *The pilot by the name of Albert Ball.*
>
> *No matter what the odds,*
> *He left his fate up to the gods,*
> *Laughing as the bullets brushed his skin.*
> *Like a medieval knight,*
> *He would charge into the fight*
> *And trust that one more time his pluck would let him*
> *   win.*
>
> *So he courted the reaper,*
> *Like the woman of his dreams,*
> *And the reaper smiled each time he came to call;*
> *But the British like their heroes*
> *Cold and dead, or so it seems,*
> *And their hero in the sky was Albert Ball.*
>
> *But long after the fight,*
> *Way into the night,*
> *Cold thoughts, as dark as night, would fill his brain,*
> *For bloodstains never fade,*
> *And there are debts to be repaid*
> *For the souls of all those men who died in vain.*

So when the night was dark and deep,
And the men lay fast asleep,
An eerie sound would filter through the night.
It was a violin,
A sound as soft as skin.
Someone was playing in the dim moonlight.

There he stood, dark and thin,
And on his violin
Played a song that spoke of loneliness and pain.
It mourned his victories;
It mourned dead enemies
And friends that he would never see again.

Yes, he courted the reaper,
Like the woman of his dreams,
And the reaper smiled each time he came to call;
But the British like their heroes
Cold and dead, or so it seems,
And their hero in the sky was Albert Ball.

It's an ironic twist of fate
That brings a hero to the gate,
And Ball was no exception to that rule;
Fate puts out the spark
In a way as if to mark
The fine line between a hero and a fool.

Each time he crossed the line,
Albert Ball would check the time
By an old church clock reminding him of home.
The Huns came to know
The man who flew so low
On his way back to the aerodrome.

It was the sixth of May,
He'd done bloody well that day;
For the forty-fourth time, he'd won the game.
As he flew low to check the hour,
A hail of bullets from the tower —
And Albert Ball lay dying in the flames.

But through his clouded eyes,
Maybe he realized,
This was the moment he'd been waiting for.
For the moment that he died,
He was a hero, bonafide.
There are to be no living heroes in this war.

For when a country goes insane,
Obsessed with blood and pain,
Just to be alive is something of a sin.
A war's not satisfied
Until all the best have died,
And the devil take the man who saves his skin.

But sometimes late at night,
When the moon is cold and bright,
I sometimes think I hear that violin.
Death is waiting just outside,
And my eyes are open wide,
As I lie and wait for morning to begin.

Now I am courting the reaper,
Like the woman of my dreams,
And the reaper smiles each time I come to call;
But the British like their heroes
Cold and dead, or so it seems,
And my name will take the place of Albert Ball.

The PIANO PLAYER sings a sad song.
BISHOP joins in.

BISHOP AND PIANO PLAYER: *singing*

> Look at the names on the statues
> Everywhere you go.
> Someone was killed
> A long time ago.
> I remember the faces;
> I remember the time.
> Those were the names of friends of mine.

> The statues are old now
> And they're fading fast.
> Something big must have happened
> Way in the past.
> The names are so faded
> You can hardly see,
> But the faces are always young to me.

Chorus

> Friends ain't s'posed to die
> 'Til they're old.
> And friends ain't s'posed to die
> In pain.
> No one should die alone
> When he is twenty-one,
> And living shouldn't make you feel ashamed.

> I can't believe
> How young we were back then.
> One thing's for sure,
> We'll never be that young again.
> We were daring young men,
> With hearts of gold,
> And most of us never got old.

In an abrupt change of mood, a loud pounding is heard. CEDRIC is knocking on BISHOP's door.

CEDRIC:
> Wakey, wakey, Bishop. Rise, man! Rise and shine!

BISHOP is hung over.

BISHOP:
> Ohhhh, Cedric. What's the idea of waking me up in the middle of the night?

CEDRIC:
> It's bloody well eleven o'clock and Madam has a bone to pick with you.

BISHOP:
> All right, all right, I'll be right there.

Pause.

Good morning, Granny.

LADY ST. HELIER:
> Bishop! Sit down. I have a bone to pick with you. Cedric, the colonial is under the weather. Bring tea and Epsom salts. Where were you last night, Bishop?

BISHOP:
> I was out.

LADY ST. HELIER:
> Good. Very specific. Well, I have my own sources and the picture that was painted for me is not fit for public viewing. Disgusting, unmannered and informal practices in company

which is unworthy, even of you, Bishop. But
what concerns me is not where you were, but
where you were not. To wit, you were not at a
party which I personally arranged, at which you
were to meet Bonar Law, Chancellor of the
Exchequer. What do you have to say in your
defence?

BISHOP:
Look, Granny. . . .

LADY ST. HELIER:
I'll thank you not to call me Granny. The
quaintness quite turns my stomach.

BISHOP:
Look, that was the fourth darn formal dinner
this week! First, it's General Haigh, then
what's-his-name, the Parliamentary
Secretary. . . . I want to have some fun!

LADY ST. HELIER:
Bishop, I'm only going to say this once. It is not
for you to be interested, amused or entertained.
You are no longer a rather short Canadian with
bad taste and a poor service record. You are a
figurehead, unlikely as that may seem. A
dignitary. The people of Canada, England, the
Empire; indeed, the world, look to you as a
symbol of victory and you will act the part. You
will shine your shoes and press your trousers.
You will refrain from spitting, swearing,
gambling and public drunkenness, and you will,
and I say this with emphasis, you will keep your
appointments with your betters. Now, tonight
you are having dinner with Lord Beaverbrook,
and tomorrow night, with Attorney-General
F.E. Smith. Need I say more?

BISHOP:

No, no. I'll be there.

LADY ST. HELIER:

Good. Oh, and Bishop, I had the occasion to
pass the upstairs bathroom this morning and I
took the liberty of inspecting your toilet kit.
There is what I can only describe as moss
growing on your hairbrush and your after shave
lotion has the odour of cat urine. I believe the
implications are clear.

Addressing the butler.

Cedric, a difficult road lies before us. Empire
must rely for its defences upon an assemblage of
Canadians, Australians and Blacks. And now,
the Americans. Our way of life is in peril!

BISHOP: *slightly drunk and writing a letter*

Dearest Margaret. I'm not sure I can get
through this evening. In the next room is
Princess Marie-Louise and four or five Lords
and Ladies whose names I can't even remember.
I drank a little bit too much champagne at
supper tonight and told the Princess a lot of lies.
Now I'm afraid to go back in there because I
can't remember what the lies are and I'm afraid
I'll contradict myself and look like an idiot.
Being rich, you've got a lot more class than me.
They'd like you. Maybe we ought to get
married. Thinking of you constantly, I
remain....

*The PIANO PLAYER and BISHOP break into
song.*

BISHOP AND PIANO PLAYER: *singing*

> *When you steal a girl*
> *From an English Earl*
> *How can you go back home*
> *Just a Canadian boy*
> *England's pride and joy*
> *How can you go back home*
> *You may be a King on your native ground*
> *But when you go back to your own home town*
> *They'll find ways to shoot you down*
> *How can you go back home.*

> *Oh baby*
> *I'm so far from home*
> *And I'm all alone*
> *And I'm savin' England's ass*
> *And although I'm not your class*
> *I got a chest that's full of brass*
> *So won't you give me a kiss*
> *Before I hit the sky*
> *One if I live*
> *And one if I die*
> *And maybe a third before we say good-bye*
> *How can you go back home.*

Chorus

The prime of life
The best of men
It will never be
Like this again
Who wants a life
Of 'remember when'...
How can you go back home.

The music changes to a more sinister note.

The following story is half-told, half-acted out, the
overall effect being of an adventure story being told
in the present tense. It is done as a boy might tell a
story, full of his own sound effects.

BISHOP:
I woke up at three o'clock in the morning. Jeez, was
I scared! Very tense, you know? I mean, Ball said
you couldn't do it with just one guy and Ball was a
maniac. But I figure it's no more dangerous than
what we do every day, so what the hell. I mean, it's
no worse. I don't think. The trouble is, no one has
ever attacked a German aerodrome single handedly
before, so it's chancy, you know what I mean? I put
my flying suit on over my pyjamas, grab a cup of tea
and out I go. It's raining. Lousy weather for it, but
what can you do? Walter Bourne, my mechanic, is
the only other man up. He has the engine running
and waiting for me.

BOURNE:
Bloody stupid idea if you ask me, Sir. I would put
thumbs down on the whole thing and go back to bed
if I was you, Sir.

BISHOP:

>Thanks a lot, Walter. That's really encouraging.

BOURNE:

>It's pissing rain, Sir. Bleeding pity to die in the pissing rain. I can see it all now. Clear as crystal before me very eyes. First, Albert Ball snuffs it. Then, Captain Bishop snuffs it. It's a bleeding pity if you ask me, Sir. I mean, it's a ball-up from beginning to end. Why don't you take my advice and go back to bed like a good lad, Sir?

BISHOP:

>Why don't you shut up, Walter? Ready?

BOURNE:

>Ready, Sir!

>*The plane takes off.*

BISHOP:

>God, it's awful up here! Pale grey light, cold, lonely as hell. My stomach's bothering me. Nerves? Naw, forgot to eat breakfast. Shit, just something else to put up with. RRRrrrr. I climb to just inside the clouds as I go over the line. No trouble? Good. Everybody is asleep. Let's find that German aerodrome. RRrrr. Where is it? Should be right around here. RRRrrr.

>*He spots something.*

All right, a quick pass, a few bursts inside those sheds, just to wake them up, and then pick them off one by one as they try to come up. Wait a minute, wait a minute. There's no planes. There's no people. The bloody place is deserted. Well, shit, that's that, isn't it? I mean, I can't shoot anyone if there is nobody here to shoot. Bloody stupid embarrassment, that's what it is. RRrrr. Feeling really miserable now, I cruise now looking for some troops to shoot them. RRrrrr. Nobody! What the hell is going on around here? Is everybody on vacation? Suddenly, I see the sheds of another German aerodrome ahead and slightly to the left. Dandy. Trouble is, it's a little far behind the lines and I'm not exactly sure where I am. But, it's either that or go back. My stomach is really bothering me now. Why didn't I eat breakfast? And why didn't I change out of my pyjamas? That's going to be great, isn't it, if I'm taken prisoner, real dignified? Spend the rest of the bloody war in my bloody pyjamas. RRRrrrrrr. Over the aerodrome at about three hundred feet. Jeezus, we got lots of planes here, lots and lots of planes. What have we got. . . six scouts and a two-seater? Jeez, I hope that two-seater doesn't come up for me. I'll have a hell of a time getting him from the rear. It's a little late to think about it now. RRRRrrrrrr.

Machine gun fire opens up.

AKAKAKakakakak. RRRRRRRRRrrrr. AKAKAKakaka.

On the ground, GERMANS are heard yelling.

GERMANS:
Ach Himmel! In's Gelände! In's Gelände! Hier sind wir alle tot!

BISHOP:

I don't know how many guys I got on that first pass. A lot of guys went down; a lot of guys stayed down. I shot up a couple of their planes pretty bad.

The sound of ground fire is heard.

I forgot about the machine gun guarding the aerodrome, bullets all around me, tearing up the canvas on my machine. Just so long as they don't hit a wire. Keep dodging. RRrrr. RRRrrr. I can't get too far away or I'll never pick them off as they try to come up. Come on, you guys, come on! One of them is starting to taxi now. I come right down on the deck about fifteen feet behind him. AKAKAkakaka. He gets six feet off the ground, side slips, does this weird sommersault and smashes into the end of the field. I pull her around as quick as I can...RRRrrr...just in time to pick up another fellow as he tries to come up. AKAKAKAakaka. My tracers are going wide...AKAKAKA...but the guy is so frightened that he doesn't watch where he is going and smashes into some trees at the end of the field. I put a few rounds into him and pull back on the stick. RRRrrrrrr. I'm feeling great now. I don't feel scared, I don't feel nothing. Just ready to fight. Come on, you bastards, come on! Wait a minute, wait a minute. This is what Ball was worried about. Two of them are taking off in opposite directions at the same time. Now I feel scared. What do I do now? Get the hell out, that's what you do! One of them is close enough behind me to start firing. Where's the other one? Still on the ground. All right, you want to fight? We'll fight! I put it into a tight turn, he stays right with me, but not

quite tight enough. As he comes in for his second firing pass, I evade him with a lateral loop, rudder down off the top and drop on his tail...AKAKAKAKAKAKAKAK...I hit the man. The plane goes down and crashes in flames on the field. Beautiful! The second man is closing with me. I have just enough time to put on my last drum of ammunition. I fly straight for him, the old chicken game. I use up all my ammunition...AKAKAKAka...I miss him, but he doesn't want to fight. Probably thinks I'm crazy. I got to get out of here. They will have telephoned every aerodrome in the area. There will be hundreds of planes after me. I climb and head for home. RRRrrrrrr. All by myself again, at last. Am I going the right way? Yeah. Jeezus, my stomach! Sharp pains, like I've been shot. Nope, no blood. Good, I haven't been shot, it's just all that excitement on an empty stomach. Being frightened. Jeez, I think I'm going to pass out. No, don't pass out!

He looks up.

And then I look up and my heart stops dead then and there. I'm not kidding. One thousand feet above me, six Albatross scouts, and me, with no ammunition. I think I'm going to puke. No, don't puke! Fly underneath them, maybe they won't see you. RRRrrrrr. I try to keep up....For a mile, I fly underneath them, just trying to keep up. RRRrrrr. I got to get away. They're faster than me and if they see me, they got me. But I got to get away! I dive and head for the line...RRRRRRRRRR!...I can feel the bullets smashing into my back at any second, into my arms, into my legs, into my....

90

He looks up again.

Nothing! Jeez, they didn't see me. RRRRrrr.
Filescamp. Home. Just land it, take it easy.
RRRR. I land. Walter Bourne is waiting with a
group of the others.

BOURNE:

I'm standing around, waiting for him to be
phoned in missing, when there he comes. Like
he's been out sightseeing. He lands with his
usual skill, cracking both wheels, then comes to
a halt, just like usual, except there is nothing left
of his bloody machine. It's in pieces, bits of
canvas flopping around like laundry in the
breeze. Beats me how it stayed together.
Captain Bishop sits there, quiet-like, then he
turns to me and he says: "Walter," he says,
"Walter, I did it. I DID IT! Never had so much
fun in me whole life!"

BISHOP:

That was the best fight I ever had. Everyone
made a very big deal of it, but I just kept
fighting all summer. My score kept getting
higher and higher and I was feeling good. By
the middle of August, I had forty-three, just one
less than Albert Ball. And that's when the
generals and colonels started treating me funny.

Going to war music is heard once again.

TRENCHARD:

Bishop! Yes, we have lots of medals for you, eh?
Lots and lots of medals. And that's not all, no,
no, no. You will receive your medals, then you'll
go on extended Canada leave and you won't
fight again.

BISHOP:

What did you say, Sir?

TRENCHARD:

Do I have a speech impediment, Bishop? I said you won't fight again.

BISHOP:

Not fight again? But I've got to fight again. I've got forty-three; Ball had forty-four. All I need is one more of those sons of. . . .

TRENCHARD:

Bishop! You have done very well. You will receive the Victoria Cross, the Distinguished Service Order, the Military Cross. No British pilot has done that, not even Albert Ball, God rest his soul. Leave it at that, Bishop. You have done England a great service. Thank you very much. Now you don't have to fight any more. I should think you'd be delighted.

BISHOP:

You don't understand, Sir. I like it.

TRENCHARD:

Oh, I know you like it. But it's becoming something of a problem. You see, you have become a colonial figurehead.

BISHOP:

I know, a dignitary.

TRENCHARD:

A colonial dignitary, Bishop. There is a difference. You see, Bishop, the problem with your colonial is that he has a morbid enthusiasm for life. You might call it a Life-Wish. Now, what happens when your colonial figurehead gets killed? I'll tell you what happens. Colonial morale plummets. Despair is in the air. Fatalism rears it's ugly head. But a living colonial figurehead is a different cup of tea. The men are inspired. They say: "He did it and he lived. I can do it too." Do you get the picture, Bishop?

BISHOP:
I believe I do, Sir.

TRENCHARD:
Good lad. You shall leave Squadron Sixty, never to return, on the morning of August 17th. That is all.

BISHOP:
Well, that still gives me a week. A lot can be done in a week.

To the audience.

In the next six days, I shot down five planes. I really was Number One now. And the squadron, they gave me a big piss-up on my last night. But something happened in that last week that made me fairly glad to get out of it for a while. It was number forty-six.

Music is heard.

It's dusk. Around eight o'clock. I'm returning to Filescamp pretty leisurely because I figure this is my last bit of flying for a bit. It's a nice clear evening and when it's clear up there in the evening, it's really very pretty. Suddenly, I see this German Aviatic two-seater heading right for me. It's a gift. I don't even have to think about this one. I put the plane down into a steep dive and come up underneath him and just rake his belly with bullets. Well, I don't know how they built those planes, but the whole thing just fell apart right before my very eyes. The wings came off, bits of the fusilage just collapsed, and the pilot and the gunner, they fall free. Now I'm pretty sure I didn't hit them, so they are alive and there is nothing I can do to help them or shoot them or anything. All I can do is just sit there and watch those two men fall, wide awake...to die! It's awful. I know I've killed lots of them, but this is different. I can watch them falling down, down. One minute, two minutes, three minutes. It's almost like I can feel them looking at me.

He stops for a moment, perplexed by unfamiliar qualms, shrugs and then goes on.

So when I leave for London the next day, I'm pretty glad to be going after all.

The scene changes to London.

LADY ST. HELIER:
Bishop, today you will meet the King. This represents a high water mark for us all and you must see to it that you do not make a balls-up of it. I understand the King is particularly excited today. It seems this is his first opportunity of presenting three medals to the same gentleman. Furthermore, the King is amused that that gentleman is from the colonies. The King, therefore, may speak to you. Should you be so honoured, you will respond politely, in grammatically cogent phrases, with neither cloying sentimentality nor rude familiarity. You

will speak to the King with dignity and restraint. Do you think you can manage that, Bishop? Is it possible that the safest course would be for you to keep your mouth shut?

Music is heard.

BISHOP:
I arrive at Buckingham Palace, late. It is very confusing.

ADJUTANT:
Excuse me, sir, but where do you think you're going?

BISHOP:
Oh, look, I'm supposed to get a medal or something around here.

ADJUTANT:
Oh, you're way off, you are, sir. This is His Majesty's personal reception area. You just about stumbled into the royal loo!!!

2ND OFFICER:
What seems to be the trouble around here?

ADJUTANT:
Good Lord! Well, the colonial here wants a medal, but his sense of direction seems to have failed him.

2ND OFFICER:
Come along, Bishop. We've been looking all over for you. Now, the procedure is this: ten paces to the centre, turn, bow.

The music strikes up "Land of Hope and Glory."

It's started already, Bishop. You're just going to have to wing it!

The music continues as a processional. BISHOP enters stiffly into the presence of the King.

BISHOP:

Here comes the King with his retinue, Order of St. Michael, Order of St. George, and here I am. The King pins three medals on my chest. Then he says. . . .

The King's voice is booming, echoing. It is spoken by the PIANO PLAYER and mimed by BISHOP.

PIANO PLAYER:

Well, Captain Bishop. You've been a busy bugger!

BISHOP:

I'm not kidding. I'm standing here and the King is standing here. The King talks to me for fifteen minutes! I can't say a word. I've lost my voice. But after the investiture comes the parties, the balls, the photographers, the newspaper reporters, the Lords and Ladies, the champagne, the filet mignon and the fifty-year-old brandy. And here's me, Billy Bishop, from Owen Sound, Canada, and I know one thing: this is my day! There will never be a day like it! I think of this as we dance far into the night, as we dance to the music of. . .the Empire Soirée.

The PIANO PLAYER and BISHOP sing sotto
and sinister.

BISHOP AND PIANO PLAYER: *singing*
 Civilizations come and go, (don't you know),
 Dancing on to oblivion (oblivion).
 The birth and death of nations,
 Of civilizations,
 Can be viewed down the barrel of a gun.

 Nobody knows who calls the tune, (calls the tune),
 It's been on the Hit Parade for many years, (can't
   you hear).
 You and I must join the chorus,
 Like ancestors before us,
 And like them, we're going to disappear.

 Chorus

 You're all invited to the Empire Soirée,
 We'll see each other there, just wait and see;
 Attendance is required at the Empire Soirée,
 We'll all dance the dance of history.

 Revolutions come and go, (don't you know).
 New empires will take the other's place, (take their
   place).
 The song may be fun,
 But a new dance has begun,
 When someone points a gun at someone's face.

 Alexander and Julius had their dance, (had their
   chance),
 'Til somebody said: "May I cut in?" (with a grin).
 All you and I can do,
 Is put on our dancing shoes,
 And wait for the next one to begin.

Chorus

You're all invited to the Empire Soirée,
We'll see each other there, just wait and see;
Attendance is required at the Empire Soirée,
We'll all dance the dance of history.

> *At the end of "The Empire Soirée," BISHOP does*
> *a little dance of victory for the audience, ending*
> *with a final salute.*

> *Blackout.*

> *A spotlight hits the PIANO PLAYER, who sings*
> *a narration summing up BISHOP's career and*
> *building to a reprise of "We Were Off to Fight the*
> *Hun." The song has a bitter edge now, for it is*
> *World War II we are talking about.*

PIANO PLAYER: *singing*
Billy went back home again,
But still, he was not done;
Seventy-two planes did their dance,
To the rhythm of his guns.
And in twenty years, he was back again,
A new war to be won;
And the hero calls to new recruits in 1941.
The hero calls to new recruits in 1941.

And they were off to fight the Hun,
They would shoot him with a gun.
Their medals would shine,
Like a sabre in the sun.
They were off to fight the Hun
And it looked like lots of fun,
Somehow it didn't seem like war
At all, at all, at all.
Somehow it didn't seem like war at all.

The lights come up slowly on BISHOP. Twenty years have gone by and he is much older and very tired. He is wearing an astonishing array of medals and they seem to weigh him down a bit.

BISHOP addresses the audience as though they were fresh World War II recruits. His voice has the tone and melody of war rhetoric.

The PIANO PLAYER plays "God Save the King."

BISHOP:
I have seen you go and my heart is very proud. Once again, in the brief space of twenty years, our brave young men rush to the defence of the Mother Country. Once again, you must go forward with all the courage and vigour of youth to wrest mankind from the grip of the Iron Cross and the Swastika. Once again, on the edge of destiny, you must test your strength. I know you of old, I think. God speed you. God speed you, the Army, on feet and on wheels, a member of which I was for so many happy years of my life. God speed you the Air Force, where in the crucible of battle, I grew from youth to manhood. God speed you and God bless you. For, once again, the freedom of mankind rests in you: in the courage, the skill, the strength and the blood of our indomitable youth.

BISHOP's recruitment speech ends on a grand note. He stops and stares at the audience for a while with a certain amount of bewilderment. The PIANO PLAYER plays a haunting and discordant "In the Sky." BISHOP speaks, but this time it is quiet and personal.

You know, I pinned the wings on my own son this week. Margaret and I are very proud of him. And of our daughter. Three Bishops in uniform fighting the same war. Well, I guess I'm on the sidelines cheering them on. It comes as a bit of a surprise to me that there is another war on. We didn't think there was going to be another one back in 1918. Makes you wonder what it was all for? But then, we're not in control of any of these things, are we? And all in all. I would have to say, it was a hell of a time!

BILLY BISHOP sings a cappella.

BISHOP: *singing*
Oh, the bloody earth is littered,
With the fighters and the quitters.
You can hear the soldiers yearning:
"Oh, if only I could fly!"
From the burning sun, I'll sight you,
In the burning sun, I'll fight you,
Oh, let us dance together in the sky.

The PIANO PLAYER joins him in the chorus.

BISHOP AND PIANO PLAYER: *singing*
In the sky,
In the sky,
Just you and I up there together,
Who knows why?
One the hunter, one the hunted;
A life to live, a death confronted.
Oh, let us dance together in the sky.

BISHOP:
Goodnight, ladies. Goodnight, gentlemen.
Goodnight.

Blackout.

Colours in the Dark - James Reaney
The Ecstasy of Rita Joe - George Ryga
Captives of the Faceless Drummer - George Ryga
Crabdance - Beverley Simons
Listen to the Wind - James Reaney
Esker Mike & His Wife, Agiluk - Herschel Hardin
Sunrise on Sarah - George Ryga
Walsh - Sharon Pollock
The Factory Lab Anthology - Connie Brissenden, ed.
Battering Ram - David Freeman
Hosanna - Michel Tremblay
Les Belles Soeurs - Michel Tremblay
API 2967 - Robert Gurik
You're Gonna Be Alright Jamie Boy - David Freeman
Bethune - Rod Langley
Preparing - Beverley Simons
Forever Yours Marie-Lou - Michel Tremblay
En Pièces Détachées - Michel Tremblay
Lulu Street - Ann Henry
Three Plays by Eric Nicol - Eric Nicol
Fifteen Miles of Broken Glass - Tom Hendry
Bonjour, là, Bonjour - Michel Tremblay
Jacob's Wake - Michael Cook
On the Job - David Fennario
Sqrieux-de-Dieu - Betty Lambert
Some Angry Summer Songs - John Herbert
The Execution - Marie-Claire Blais
Tiln & Other Plays - Michael Cook
The Great Wave of Civilization - Herschel Hardin
La Duchesse de Langeais & Other Plays - Michel Tremblay
Have - Julius Hay
Cruel Tears - Ken Mitchell and Humphrey & the Dumptrucks
Ploughmen of the Glacier - George Ryga
Nothing to Lose - David Fennario
Les Canadiens - Rick Salutin
Seven Hours to Sundown - George Ryga
Can You See Me Yet? - Timothy Findley
Two Plays - George Woodcock
Ashes - David Rudkin
Spratt - Joe Wiesenfeld
Walls - Christian Bruyere
Boiler Room Suite - Rex Deverell
Angel City, Curse of the Starving Class & Other Plays - Sam Shepard
Buried Child & Other Plays - Sam Shepard
The Primary English Class - Israel Horovitz
Mackerel - Israel Horovitz
Jitters - David French
Aléola - Gaëtan Charlebois
After Abraham - Ron Chudley
The Lionel Touch - George Hulme
Sainte-Marie Among the Hurons - James W. Nichol

Balconville - David Fennario
Maggie & Pierre - Linda Griffiths with Paul Thompson
Waiting for the Parade - John Murrell
The Twilight Dinner & Other Plays - Lennox Brown
Sainte-Carmen of the Main - Michel Tremblay
Damnée Manon, Sacrée Sandra - Michel Tremblay
The Impromptu of Outremont - Michel Tremblay
Billy Bishop Goes to War - John Gray and Eric Peterson

TALONBOOKS — THEATRE FOR THE YOUNG

Raft Baby - Dennis Foon
The Windigo - Dennis Foon
Heracles - Dennis Foon
A Chain of Words - Irene N. Watts
Apple Butter - James Reaney
Geography Match - James Reaney
Names and Nicknames - James Reaney
Ignoramus - James Reaney
A Teacher's Guide to Theatre for Young People - Jane Howard Baker
A Mirror of Our Dreams - Joyce Doolittle and Zina Barnieh